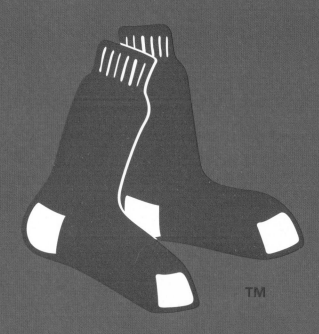

™

Wally The Green Monster™
And His Journey Through
Red Sox Nation™

Jerry Remy

Illustrated by Danny Moore

MASCOT BOOKS®
www.mascotbooks.com

It was Patriots' Day in New England and
Wally The Green Monster was celebrating
the holiday by taking a journey through
Red Sox Nation.

He started his day by running in the famous
Boston Marathon. As he ran up "Heartbreak
Hill", *Red Sox* fans cheered, "Hello, Wally!"

After the marathon, Wally hurried to *Fenway Park* for the annual Patriots' Day Red Sox game.

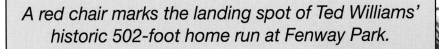

During the game, Wally entertained fans and cheered for the Red Sox. He later made his way to the press box where he visited his pal, Jerry Remy. Jerry gave Wally a high-five and said, "Hello, Wally!"

After a Red Sox victory, Wally was
off to Boston's historic Freedom Trail.

Boston Common

Starting at Boston
Common, Wally walked
along the red brick path,
stopping at each of the
sixteen landmarks on
the Freedom Trail.

Along the way, Wally learned about American history and what it was like to live in Boston over two hundred years ago.

Faneuil Hall

Bunker Hill Monument

Red Sox fans greeted Wally at every stop and cheered, "Hello, Wally!"

Other stops along the Freedom Trail include: the State House, Park Street Church, Granary Burying Ground, King's Chapel, the First Public School Site, the Old Corner Bookstore, the Old South Meeting House, Old State House, Boston Massacre Site, Paul Revere House, Old North Church, Copp's Hill Burial Ground, and the U.S.S. Constitution.

Wanting to see more of Boston,
Wally and his friends hopped into
a big tour truck and took off down
the streets of Beantown.

They visited Boston landmarks and
learned many interesting facts. Wally got
nervous when he noticed the tour truck
driving directly towards the Charles River.
With a splash, the truck drove right into
the river and turned into a boat!
Wally was amazed!

Once in the water, Wally enjoyed beautiful views of the Boston skyline. Along the way, Red Sox fans cheered, "Hello, Wally!"

Martha's Vineyard is New England's largest island.

After a day of fun in Boston, Wally headed to Cape Cod. His first stop was Martha's Vineyard, where he ran into a family of Red Sox fans near a lighthouse.

Next, Wally took a ferry to Nantucket and spent the afternoon shopping. He bought famous Nantucket baskets for a couple of his favorite Red Sox players.

Everywhere Wally went, Red Sox fans cheered, "Hello, Wally!"

Wally left Massachusetts and headed to the southern regions of Red Sox Nation, first stopping at Mystic Seaport in Connecticut.

Mystic Seaport Village was recreated to appear as it did in the 1800's.

Wally pretended to be the ship's captain as he took the helm and directed an imaginary crew.

Ready for some baseball, Wally's
next stop was historic Yale Field in
New Haven. Fans entering the ballpark
cheered, "Hello, Wally!"

Sailing is a favorite pastime of Rhode Islanders.

Wally's journey through *Red Sox Nation* took him next to Rhode Island. He climbed atop Newport Lighthouse and watched sailboats navigate the harbor. Noticing Wally on the lighthouse, sailors cheered, "Hello, Wally!"

Not wanting to miss an opportunity to see more good baseball, Wally headed to Pawtucket where he watched a Pawtucket Red Sox game.

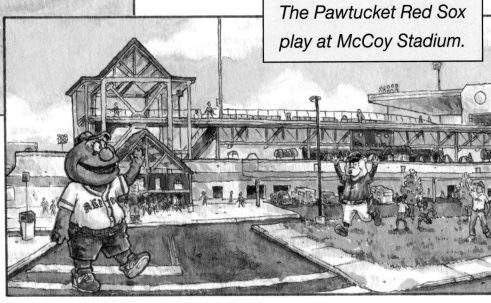

The Pawtucket Red Sox play at McCoy Stadium.

Outside the stadium, Wally ran into the Pawtucket Red Sox mascot. The two friends shared some laughs before heading into the stadium. Red Sox fans cheered, "Hello, Wally!"

It was now time for Wally to head
north to Vermont. He bundled up,
jumped on a snowboard, and hit the
slopes. The snow was unbelievable!

At 4,393 feet, Mount Mansfield is the tallest peak in the Green Mountains of Vermont.

Wally was happy to have warm
green fur on such a cold day.
As he raced down the mountain,
he ran into Red Sox fans along the
way. They cheered, "Hello, Wally!"

From the Green Mountains of
Vermont, Wally made his way to the
White Mountains of New Hampshire.
Once there, Wally hiked to the summit
of Mount Washington.

*The highest wind speed ever recorded on Earth was
231 miles per hour at the summit of Mount Washington.*

After a long climb, Wally stopped to catch his breath at the Mount Washington Observatory.
A scientist working at the Observatory taught Wally many interesting facts about the Earth's weather. From the observation deck, Wally proudly waved a Red Sox flag. The scientist cheered, "Hello, Wally!"

Maine was the final stop on Wally's journey through Red Sox Nation. With the help of a clever trap, Wally caught the biggest lobster he had ever seen. In a worried voice, the lobster said, "Hello, Wally!"

Wally wanted to see one more baseball game, so he headed to Hadlock Field, home of the Portland Sea Dogs. Wally noticed a green wall in left field similar to the *Green Monster* wall at *Fenway Park*. Seeing the wall made Wally think of his cozy home in Fenway Park.

The green wall at Hadlock Field is known as the "Maine Monster".

As Wally walked onto the field, an umpire spotted him and cheered, "Hello, Wally!"

Wally enjoyed his journey through Red Sox
Nation, but he was happy to finally be back at
Fenway Park in Boston.

While relaxing in his Adirondack chair, Wally thought about all the fun places he had visited and the many Red Sox fans he had met. He felt proud to be a part of the Red Sox family as he drifted off to sleep.

Good night, Wally.

To my favorite Wally fan, my grandson, Dominik. ~ Jerry Remy

This one is for the Hebert family, thanks for showing me true
northern hospitality. ~ Danny Moore

For more information about our products, please visit us online at www.mascotbooks.com.

Mascot Books, Inc. - P.O. Box 220157, Chantilly, VA 20153-0157

BOSTON MARATHON is a registered trademark of the Boston Athletic Association and is used with permission. PORTLAND SEA DOGS is a registered trademark of Portland Maine Baseball, Inc. and is used with permission. PAWTUCKET RED SOX is a registered trademark of Boston Red Sox Baseball Club Limited Partnership and is used with permission. Major League Baseball trademarks and copyrights are used with permission of Major League Baseball Properties, Inc.

ISBN: 978-1-932888-89-8
Printed in the United States.
www.mascotbooks.com

www.mascotbooks.com

MLB

Boston Red Sox
Hello, Wally!
by Jerry Remy

Wally's Journey Through Red Sox Nation
by Jerry Remy

New York Yankees
Let's Go, Yankees!
by Yogi Berra

New York Mets
Hello, Mr. Met!
by Rusty Staub

St. Louis Cardinals
Hello, Fredbird!
by Ozzie Smith

Chicago Cubs
Let's Go, Cubs!
by Aimee Aryal

Chicago White Sox
Hello, Southpaw!
by Aimee Aryal

Philadelphia Phillies
Hello, Phillie Phanatic!
by Aimee Aryal

Cleveland Indians
Hello, Slider!
by Bob Feller

NBA

Dallas Mavericks
Let's Go, Mavs!
by Mark Cuban

NFL

Dallas Cowboys
How 'Bout Them Cowboys!
by Aimee Aryal

More Coming Soon

Collegiate

Auburn University
War Eagle! by Pat Dye
Hello, Aubie! by Aimee Aryal

Boston College
Hello, Baldwin! by Aimee Aryal

Brigham Young University
Hello, Cosmo!
by Pat and LaVell Edwards

Clemson University
Hello, Tiger! by Aimee Aryal

Duke University
Hello, Blue Devil! by Aimee Aryal

Florida State University
Let's Go 'Noles! by Aimee Aryal

Georgia Tech
Hello, Buzz! by Aimee Aryal

Indiana University
Let's Go Hoosiers! by Aimee Aryal

James Madison University
Hello, Duke Dog! by Aimee Aryal

Kansas State University
Hello, Willie! by Dan Walter

Louisiana State University
Hello, Mike! by Aimee Aryal

Michigan State University
Hello, Sparty! by Aimee Aryal

Mississippi State University
Hello, Bully! by Aimee Aryal

North Carolina State University
Hello, Mr. Wuf! by Aimee Aryal

Penn State University
We Are Penn State by Joe Paterno
Hello, Nittany Lion! by Aimee Aryal

Purdue University
Hello, Purdue Pete! by Aimee Aryal

Rutgers University
Hello, Scarlet Knight! by Aimee Aryal

Syracuse University
Hello, Otto! by Aimee Aryal

Texas A&M
Howdy, Reveille! by Aimee Aryal

UCLA
Hello, Joe Bruin! by Aimee Aryal

University of Alabama
Roll Tide! by Kenny Stabler
Hello, Big Al! by Aimee Aryal

University of Arkansas
Hello, Big Red! By Aimee Aryal

University of Connecticut
Hello, Jonathan! by Aimee Aryal

University of Florida
Hello, Albert! by Aimee Aryal

University of Georgia
How 'Bout Them Dawgs!
by Vince Dooley
Hello, Hairy Dawg! by Aimee Aryal

University of Illinois
Let's Go, Illini! by Aimee Aryal

University of Iowa
Hello, Herky! by Aimee Aryal

University of Kansas
Hello, Big Jay! by Aimee Aryal

University of Kentucky
Hello, Wildcat! by Aimee Aryal

University of Maryland
Hello, Testudo! by Aimee Aryal

University of Michigan
Let's Go, Blue! by Aimee Aryal

University of Minnesota
Hello, Goldy! by Aimee Aryal

University of Mississippi
Hello, Colonel Rebel! by Aimee Aryal

University of Nebraska
Hello, Herbie Husker! by Aimee Aryal

University of North Carolina
Hello, Rameses! by Aimee Aryal

University of Notre Dame
Let's Go Irish! by Aimee Aryal

University of Oklahoma
Let's Go Sooners! by Aimee Aryal

University of South Carolina
Hello, Cocky! by Aimee Aryal

University of Southern California
Hello, Tommy Trojan! by Aimee Aryal

University of Tennessee
Hello, Smokey! by Aimee Aryal

University of Texas
Hello, Hook 'Em! by Aimee Aryal

University of Virginia
Hello, CavMan! by Aimee Aryal

University of Wisconsin
Hello, Bucky! by Aimee Aryal

Virginia Tech
Yea, It's Hokie Game Day!
by Cheryl and Frank Beamer
Hello, Hokie Bird! by Aimee Aryal

Wake Forest University
Hello, Demon Deacon!
by Aimee Aryal

West Virginia University
Hello, Mountaineer! by Aimee Aryal

NHL

Coming Soon

Visit us online at www.mascotbooks.com for a complete list of titles.

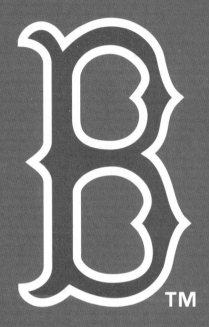